OLD HANNIBAL
and the
HURRICANE

Berthe Amoss

Hyperion Books
for
Children

Library of Congress Cataloging-in-Publication Data
Amoss, Berthe.
Old Hannibal and the hurricane / written and illustrated by Berthe
Amoss.—1st ed.
p.   cm.
Summary: On board the ship Sally Sue, Old Hannibal is describing
for his friends the great hurricane he once endured, when they run
into another one.
ISBN 1-56282-097-4 (trade)—ISBN 1-56282-098-2 (library)
[1. Hurricanes—Fiction.   2. Sea stories.] I. Title.
PZ7.A51770j 1991
[E]—dc20   91-71387   CIP
                                 AC

—for Christopher—

Jolly stories, jolly told
When the winds is bleak and the nights is cold;
No such life can be led on the shore
As is had on the rocks by the ocean's roar.

English folk song

It was a blustery day down by the sea. Fluffy clouds raced across the sky at a clip, and the air smelled of salt and fish. Matt and Sophie were helping Old Hannibal launch Sally Sue.

"Avast and away mates!" said Old Hannibal, shoving Sally Sue toward the water. "What a day for fishing!"

"But Old Hannibal," said Matt, "I see a storm cloud on the horizon."

"Never fear, Matt my boy! Remember what the Old Salts say: 'When the wind is in the east, 'tis neither good for man or beast, but when the wind is in the south, it blows the bait in the fish's mouth!'"

"Yes, but Old Hannibal," said Sophie, "you told me the Old Salts also say, 'Red sky in the morning, sailor take warning,' and look at the sky!"

"A mere pink, Sophie my girl, and Sally Sue's as sturdy a ship as ever sailed the seven seas! Heave-ho on that rope, me hearties! Single up all lines and stand by to board! A spot of heavy weather won't stop Sue and me!"

Matt tugged, Sophie shoved, and Sally Sue inched forward against the wind.

"Old Hannibal," Matt asked, "were you and Sally Sue ever in a storm at sea?"

"Were we ever in a storm at sea! Why, laddie, we were in *the* storm at sea! The biggest, blowingest, most blustering blast that ever blew! A hurricane of tremendous fame, and Bellowing Bertha was her name."

"What was it like, Old Hannibal?" Sophie asked.

"Well, mates, it began like this," said Old Hannibal, "Picture the two of you with me and Sally Sue.

"On a day when some might hug the hearth, we raised anchor and cast off. We skimmed with ease among the rocks and over the water until the waves were mountains and the troughs deep valleys.

"The sky turned dark; the wind began to wail and whine. It was Bellowing Bertha being born! She breathed and blew, she groaned and grew and howled and yowled."

You-oo! You and Sue-oo!
I'll sink you into the briny blue-oo!
"Bertha dumped seawater in our hull and threw a great wave at our stern.

"Down we went into the deep, where Neptune rules his kingdom, where white whales wallow, and silver sharks slither in and out of Davy Jones's Locker on the very floor of the ocean!

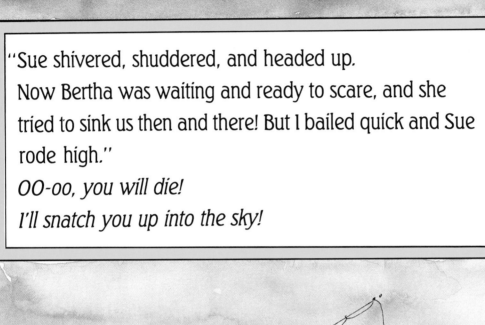

"Sue shivered, shuddered, and headed up.
Now Bertha was waiting and ready to scare, and she tried to sink us then and there! But I bailed quick and Sue rode high."

OO-oo, you will die!
I'll snatch you up into the sky!

"Up we went with everything else, with other boats and fishing floats, with buoys and barges, clippers and kippers, with trees and debris, flotsam and jetsam, and even then some!"

"Bertha tossed us stern over starboard and bow over larboard, whirling 'round upside down, and land was far away. But I thought hard and saw my chance. I reached out here and gathered there and found just what I needed.

"I hammered,

tacked,

sawed,

and made–

The Sally Sue-per sailing ship!

"Now Bertha was mad and greedy for more, and she gobbled up everything as she raced ashore. Then she grew too fat and was thirsty for sea, but she'd left that far behind. So there we were, too high in the sky with Bellowing Bertha ready to die!"

Oh woe, I'm feeling low!
Why I can hardly even blow!
Land's not so good for me-ee!
"Now I thought fast and threw out our ballast, and we glided to
rest on the very next crest.

"But hurry, lad! The glass is falling! Batten down the hatches, lassie, and toss out the anchor! It's Bertha's baby being born!"

Huff! PUFF! I'm learning to blow!
Woo-OOO! See what I do!
I stir up the sea, BUT—I can't budge Sue!
Whew! Phew!...

"She's fast to yonder stake, mates!" Old Hannibal said. "We'll
ride this one out safe and snug in Sally Sue by the sea!"
And they did.